CIP data for this title is available from the Library of Congress

ISBN 0-525-65241-8

Published in the United States by Cobblehill Books, an affiliate of Dutton Children's Book, a division of Penguin USA Inc., 375 Hudson Street, New York, New York 10014

Conceived and produced by Breslich & Foss, London

Project editor: Janet Ravenscroft
Designer: Brian Wall
Additional artwork: Anthony Duke
Photography: David Armstrong

Printed in Hong Kong

First edition 10 9 8 7 6 5 4 3 2 1

PICTURE CREDITS

Breslich & Foss are grateful to the following individuals and institutions for permission to reproduce illustrations: Bridgeman Art Library, London/Bibliotheque de Chantilly: p.24 (top); /British Library, London: p.12 (bottom), p.15 (both), p.16 (both), p.18 (top), p.19 (left and center), p.20 (top), p.21, p.27 (center), p.29 (both); /British Museum, London: p.24 (left); /Bibliotheque Nationale, Paris: p.2 (top), p.7 (left), p.13, p.20 (bottom), p.27 (left); /Giraudon: p.2 (bottom), p.17; /Lambeth Palace Library, London: p.25 (left); /Tallow Chandlers' Company, London: p.10 (center right). The Board of Trustees of the Armouries: p.3, p.5 (left), p.23 (top). Bodleian Library, Oxford: (MS. Bodl. 264, fol. 100r) p.6 (bottom), (MS. Douce 195, fol. 7r) p.24. British Library: p.5 (bottom), p.7 (right), p.18 (bottom), p.23 (bottom). E.T Archive/Burgerbibliothek, Bern: p.5 (right); /Victoria & Albert Museum, London: p.6 (top); /Trinity College, Cambridge: p.8 (bottom); /Civic Library, Padua: p.10 (top); /University Library, Heidelberg: p.10 (bottom); /Bibliotheque Nationale, Paris p.12 (top). The Fotomas Index: p.8 (top), p.25 (right). Robert Harding Picture Library: p.27 (top); /Bibliotheque Nationale p19 (right).

Jacket foreground courtesy of The Board of Trustees of the Armouries; background: Bridgeman Art Library/British Library. Endpapers: The Fotomas Index.

THE
Knight's
HANDBOOK

HOW TO BECOME A CHAMPION IN SHINING ARMOR

CHRISTOPHER GRAVETT

Cobblehill Books
Dutton New York

ARMOR AND WEAPONS

reat lords and kings needed knights to help them defend their lands, and wage war on their rivals. In battle, knights charged with their lances lowered, knocking the opposing knights from their horses.

COATS OF MAIL

nly knights could usually afford to keep several horses and wear full armor. The earliest knights wore coats of "mail" that weighed about 15 kg (33 lb). Mail was made from thousands of iron rings, each one linked to four others, and closed by a tiny rivet. By adding or removing rings, the coat could be tailored like a suit. From the twelfth century, knights wore long mail sleeves that went over the hands like mittens, and mail leggings. The coat of mail had to be flexible so that the knight could move easily.

Under their surcoats, these French knights are wearing a mixture of mail and plate armor

To make it more comfortable, a padded garment was often worn underneath. This also cushioned heavy blows from weapons. Over their armor, knights began to wear a cloth "surcoat" or tunic, sometimes decorated with their coat-of-arms.

THE HELMET

At first, the only armor made from solid steel plates was the helmet. This was usually conical, with a noseguard to protect the face from slashing blows. By about 1200, some knights were using helmets fitted with a face-mask. These developed into the "helm," which covered the whole head, and had eyeslits and breathing holes. In the fourteenth and early fifteenth centuries, knights wore a type of helmet called a "basinet." Because of the visor's strange shape, this helmet was known as a "hound's hood!"

DEADLY SPIKES

Sharp weapons tended to skid off the smooth steel plates, so weapons with spikes were used to pierce the metal, and heavy iron clubs, called maces, were used to crush or

READY FOR THE FIGHT!

What the well-dressed knight and his horse wear when going to battle

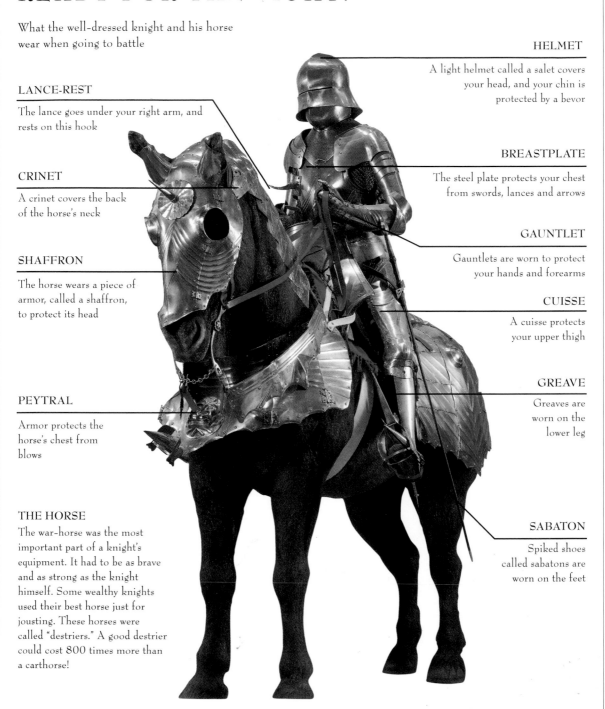

LANCE-REST

The lance goes under your right arm, and rests on this hook

CRINET

A crinet covers the back of the horse's neck

SHAFFRON

The horse wears a piece of armor, called a shaffron, to protect its head

PEYTRAL

Armor protects the horse's chest from blows

THE HORSE

The war-horse was the most important part of a knight's equipment. It had to be as brave and as strong as the knight himself. Some wealthy knights used their best horse just for jousting. These horses were called "destriers." A good destrier could cost 800 times more than a carthorse!

HELMET

A light helmet called a salet covers your head, and your chin is protected by a bevor

BREASTPLATE

The steel plate protects your chest from swords, lances and arrows

GAUNTLET

Gauntlets are worn to protect your hands and forearms

CUISSE

A cuisse protects your upper thigh

GREAVE

Greaves are worn on the lower leg

SABATON

Spiked shoes called sabatons are worn on the feet

MAKING A HELMET

Wear this helmet with your shield and sword, and you'll be ready for action!

WHAT YOU WILL NEED:

- Pencil
- Ruler
- Foil board 61 x 51 cm (2 ft x 20 in)
- Craft knife (TAKE CARE)
- Glue
- Prong paper fasteners
- Cookie cutter

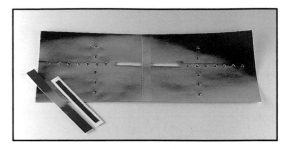

3. Cut a strip of foil board 2.5 x 20.5 cm (1 x 8 in). Place the slot from step 1 in the center and trace around it. Cut away the middle and discard. Glue across the gap in the helmet. Glue a strip 2.5 x 27 cm (1 x 10½ in) down the front.

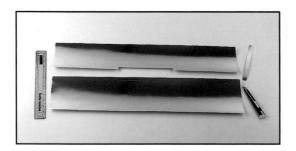

1. On your piece of foil board, draw one rectangle 61 x 12.5 cm (2 ft x 5 in) and another 61 x 15 cm (2 ft x 6 in). Cut them out. Draw a slot 17.5 x 13 mm (7 x ½ in) in the middle of one long edge of each rectangle. Cut out the slots and keep one to use in step 3.

4. Decorate the sides with more prong paper fasteners. Bend the foil board around, overlapping it at the back to make a cylinder. Glue in position.

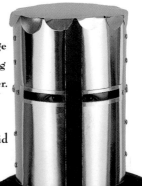

Trace around the helmet, then draw scallops along the edge of the circle by tracing around a cookie cutter. Carefully cut out the lid. Bend down each scallop and glue the lid to the helmet.

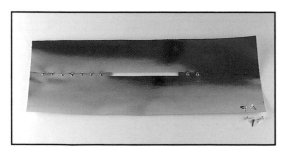

2. Overlap the two pieces of foil board and glue them together to make a gap to see through. Make tiny cuts along the glued edges, then push a prong paper fastener through each one. Open them out.

crack the armor. Cannon, then handguns, appeared on the scene in the fourteenth century, and by the seventeenth century these would help to drive the knight from the battlefield forever.

SUITS OF STEEL

Mail was strong, but it could be pierced by sharp weapons, so to protect themselves further, fourteenth-century knights began to wear a "coat of plates" over their mail. This was a sleeveless cloth garment lined with steel plates. Sometimes a solid breastplate would be attached to protect the chest, and the arms and legs were also covered in plate.

Later, the plates were worn uncovered, and held together by rivets, leather straps, buckles, and laces. By 1400, wealthy knights were clad from head to toe in shining metal.

HIGH FASHION

Armorers (the people who made the armor) gave the steel plates a fashionable shape, and some were beautifully decorated.

The knight in his armor was no match for guns and cannon

A knight's suit was specially made for him, but it would still have cost less than his best war-horse.

CARTWHEELS

The suit of armor weighed less than the pack a modern soldier carries on his back, and knights in full armor could easily mount their horses. Some knights even boasted that they could turn cartwheels, or leap into the saddle!

An iron-clad knight says good-bye to his family. A piece of armor called a shaffron protects the horse's head

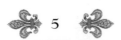

BECOMING A KNIGHT

It took a lot of hard work before a young noble could become a knight. When he was about seven years old, the boy joined a lord's household as a page. Next he would become a squire, and eventually, a knight.

FROM PAGE TO SQUIRE

In his new home, the page would run errands, learn to recite poetry, sing or play songs, and play games with the ladies. He learned how to carve meat correctly, which was considered an important skill in a lord's household. The page was also taught how to handle and clean all kinds of weapons, and how to wear armor. If he had done well, by the age of about fourteen he was ready to become a squire.

As a squire he was apprenticed to a knight. Now, as well as carrying out all his earlier duties, he learned the hunting skills required by a young noble, such as how to cut up a deer killed during a hunt, and the rules of hawking. He practiced fighting with full-sized weapons and with extra-heavy ones to build up his muscles. He learned to ride a war-horse and to control it with his legs when his hands were busy with his shield and a lance, a sword, or a heavy club called a mace.

One of the squire's most important duties was to help his master put on his armor. The brave young squire would then ride into battle by his side so that he could help the knight if he was knocked from his horse. The squire would also attend tournaments to learn the rules and help his master.

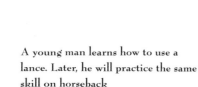

A young man learns how to use a lance. Later, he will practice the same skill on horseback

FROM SQUIRE TO KNIGHT

Usually between the ages of eighteen and twenty-one, the squire was knighted. After spending a night in church praying, he took a purifying bath. Then he received his gilded spurs, and his sword was belted to him. Finally, he was given a blow with an open hand, called a "buffet," or a tap on the shoulder with a sword by another knight, or even the king.

Once knighted, the young man had to find a way to earn a living. He might look for a rich girl to marry, or try to make his fortune competing in tournaments. Alternatively, he could hire himself out to a lord who would employ him to fight in battles, act as an escort, or represent him in the law courts.

ENEMY ATTACKS

Lords tried to avoid going into battle, especially if they were a great noble or a king, because of the risk of losing their wealth and position. They preferred to send their men to attack the enemy's villages, steal his animals and destroy his crops. In medieval times, people grew most of the food they needed at home. If all the crops were destroyed, there would be no grain to make bread, no grapes to make wine, and nothing to take to market. The villagers could starve, and the lord would lose his income.

INTO BATTLE!

The knight's training was to prepare him to fight in ferocious and bloody battles. Early knights used to gallop toward their enemy in groups, sometimes stabbing with their lances, or throwing them like spears. Others tucked them under their right arm: the knight was held so securely by his high saddle and long stirrups that the weight of the galloping horse was transferred to the point of his lance. By about 1100, all knights fought like this.

Knights fight on foot with swords and heavy axes

Galloping knights charge the enemy with their lances lowered

A solid line of mounted knights with their lances straight out in front formed a deadly wall of spikes. Once the knights had crashed through the enemy line, their lances were often broken and useless, so they drew their swords to continue the fight.

Archers, sometimes protected behind sharp stakes, shot clouds of arrows at the knights. Solid masses of men with long spears, or even longer pikes, could form a dense "porcupine" of points that the horses could not break.

In the fifteenth century, some eastern European soldiers defended themselves behind wagons, and shot at knights with cannon and handguns.

Wars could last for years on end, and while the knight was away fighting, his lady was left in charge of the household. If the castle was attacked or besieged, the lady would have to defend it from the enemy.

MEDIEVAL MEDICINE

If a knight was injured in battle, the doctor would seal the blood vessels with a red-hot brand or boiling oil! Some doctors used bandages soaked in egg white to soothe minor injuries. Small wounds could be stitched up and some healed, but most were fatal. Many knights dislocated their shoulders by falling off their horses, and had to have them pulled back into their sockets.

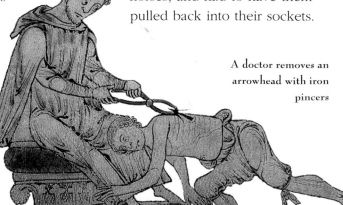

A doctor removes an arrowhead with iron pincers

MAKING A KNIGHTLY SWORD

The most important part of a knight's equipment—apart from his horse—was his sword. Follow this pattern to make your own.

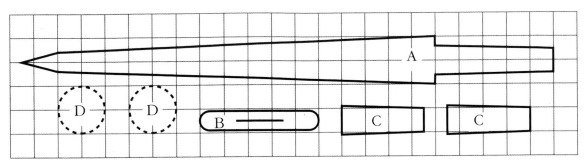

On cardboard, draw a grid four times as big as the one shown. One square should equal 2.5 cm (1 in).

WHAT YOU WILL NEED:

- Pencil
- Ruler
- Thin cardboard 61 x 15 cm (2 ft x 6 in)
- Scissors
- Aluminum foil
- Glue
- Black tape
- Jar lid

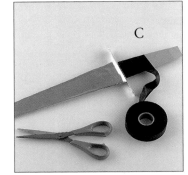

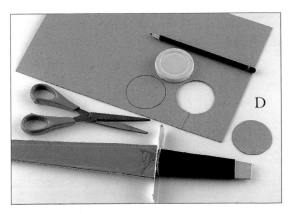

2. Cut a slit in the handguard (B) and slide it over the handle. Glue the grips (C) to the sides of the handle. Wrap them in black tape.

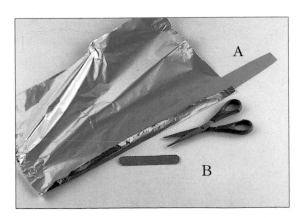

1. Draw parts A-C on your enlarged grid. Cut them out. Cover both sides of the blade (A) and both sides of the handguard (B) with foil. Glue in place.

3. To make a pommel (D), draw two circles by tracing around a jar lid. Cut the circles out and glue them over the end of the handle. Cover the pommel with foil.

HERALDRY

In the twelfth century, knights began to wear special patterns so that they could be recognized at contests and in battle. The code that controlled who could have which shapes and colors is called "heraldry."

COATS-OF-ARMS

A knight often wore his family's design on his cloth tunic or "surcoat," and this is what gave us the term "coat-of-arms." The knight's horse was dressed in a long covering called a "trapper," which was decorated with the knight's design. The coat-of-arms would also be painted on the knight's shield, and on a flag called a "banner." The knight's wife and family could use the coat-of-arms on their clothes and possessions, too.

HERALDIC COLORS

Knights chose all sorts of designs for their coats-of-arms: some knights liked to have animals like lions and dolphins on their shields, others preferred geometric shapes. There were rules to prevent families from having the same arms, and to make designs easier to see. The animals had to be drawn in a certain way, and there were rules about how colors were used. Silver and gold were called "metals," and these could be placed on top of or under red, blue, black, or green. The well-dressed knight sometimes attached a colorful crest to the top of his helmet. The crest could be made from leather or wood. This made it easier for heralds and friends to identify the knight in a tournament or battle.

A BRAVE MESSENGER

"Heralds" kept records of coats-of-arms, and tried to enforce the rules. Kings and great lords had their own heralds, who wore their masters' arms on a loose coat called a "tabard." Heralds had the dangerous job of acting as messengers between courts, delivering challenges to tournaments, or even to war. Their other important duties included shouting out the names of contestants at tournaments, and identifying the dead on the battlefield by their coats-of-arms.

Knights recognized each other in battle by their coats-of-arms

MAKING A SHIELD OF ARMS

Design your own shield for going into battle!
Copy one of the traditional patterns shown here, or make up one of your own. Remember, knights wear their shield on their left arm, and carry their sword on their right.

WHAT YOU WILL NEED:

- 2 sheets of white paper, 56 x 46 cm (22 x 18 in)
- Thick cardboard, 56 x 46 cm (22 x 18 in)
- Thin cardboard, 50 x 23 cm (20 x 9 in)
- Pencil
- Scissors
- Glue
- Poster paints
- Prong paper fasteners

1. Fold a sheet of paper in half lengthways. Draw a curving line from the middle of the outside edge to the bottom of the fold. Cut along the line, open up the paper, and you will have a shield shape.

2. Lay the shape over the cardboard and trace around it. Remove the pattern and cut out the cardboard shield. Lay the pattern on the second sheet of paper and cut out another shield shape.

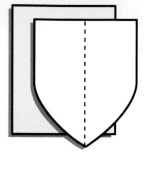

3. Glue the second sheet of paper to the cardboard shield. Draw and paint your coat-of-arms. Knights were fond of lions and eagles, fleur-de-lys, stars, cockleshells, and geometric designs. Don't forget the rules about color!

4. Cut three strips of thin cardboard about 8 cm (3 in) wide. Hold your left arm against the back of the shield, your fist toward the top right-hand corner. Make a mark on the shield where the strips should go. Make a small hole in both ends of each strip and in the shield. Push the prong paper fasteners through the front of the shield and open them out at the back.

THE CASTLE AND MANOR

Castles were often built on hillsides overlooking rivers, from where the lord's soldiers could keep watch over the surrounding country. When not at a castle, lords lived in their manor houses.

EARTH AND TIMBER

The first castles were probably built in France in the ninth or tenth centuries, by lords keen to protect themselves from their enemies. These castles were usually simple enclosures protected by timber fences and surrounded by a ditch. In the eleventh century, "motte and bailey" castles become common. The motte was an earthen mound

A siege tower

The attackers of this castle try to destroy the walls with cannon, while crossbowmen shoot at the men inside

Joan of Arc, a French leader, urges her archers to shoot at the enemy behind the battlements. The soldiers try to build a bridge, so they can cross the moat

with a timber tower on top. The "bailey" was the defended courtyard that held stables, barns, workshops, and sometimes the great hall in which the lord and his household ate their meals.

A COZY KEEP

Earth and timber castles were easy to build, but they were also easy to burn down. By the twelfth century, wealthy lords made their castles safer and more comfortable by adding a separate stone tower or "keep." The walls of the keep were very thick—sometimes 6 meters (19½ feet) thick at the base!—which

made them difficult to break down. The keep had a basement store, an entrance on the first floor for security, and other rooms above. The walls of these rooms were hung with tapestries, or painted to brighten them.

ROUND TOWERS AND FIERCE ARCHERS

Archers defending the corners of a keep risked being shot whenever they poked their heads beyond the battlements. It was also easy for an enemy to tunnel under the corner of a keep and bring down the walls. At the end of the twelfth century, round keeps

MAKING A CASTLE

Build a traditional stone castle with battlements, a drawbridge, and tall towers.
Rub the plastic bottles with sandpaper first, so that the paint will stick to them.

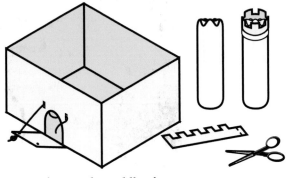

WHAT YOU WILL NEED:

- Cardboard box
- Thin cardboard
- Pencil
- Scissors or craft knife
- Masking tape
- String
- 4 large plastic soda bottles
- Poster paints

1. Draw and cut out a door in the middle of one
side of the box. On cardboard, draw a rectangle
just bigger than the door. Cut it out and tape one
edge under the box. Make two holes in the card
and two slots above the door. Knot the end of a
piece of string then thread it through one hole and
through the slots. Thread the loose end through
the last hole and knot it, leaving a loop inside the
box. Cut the tops off the plastic bottles and turn
them upside down. Measure their circumference.
Draw and cut out battlements. Tape them around
the tops of the bottles.

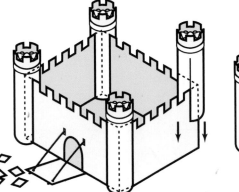

2. Cut notches around the top of the box to form
battlements. Measure the height of the box. Cut two
slots in the sides of the bottles and slot them over
the walls.

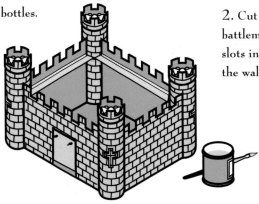

3. Paint the walls and the towers, and draw stones and
windows with a marker pen. If you like, tape cardboard
walkways inside the walls, under the battlements.

appeared, and round towers were built along the walls, making the castle easier to defend.

Some castles had several courtyards and, by the late thirteenth century, it was popular to put one inside another, to form two rings of walls. The outer wall was lower, so archers on the inner wall could shoot over the heads of their companions in front. The entrance to the castle was defended on each side by a tower, and guarded by a drawbridge, a portcullis and thick wooden doors.

RAISE THE DRAWBRIDGE!

Once the drawbridge was raised, one way to get into the castle was to tunnel under the walls—unless the castle was surrounded by a river or a "moat" (a deep ditch filled with water). The other solution was to climb over the walls using ladders. From the top of a wooden siege tower, archers could shoot their arrows into the castle, while soldiers tried to scale the walls.

Villagers farm the land in the grounds of a manor house

At the manor house, women untangle wool and spin it into yarn that will be woven into cloth

LORD OF THE MANOR

In medieval times, most land belonged to kings and other great lords. Knights were often given an estate or "manor" by their lord, in return for help in battle. A manor included one or more villages, and the peasants who lived there would have to work on the knight's farm for free. They would also have a plot of land of their own to farm.

The knight would live in his manor house when not at war, or on duty at one of the lord's castles. Many knights preferred to stay on their manors instead of going to war, where they might be killed. Some chose to send money to the lord instead of fighting themselves. With this money, the lord could buy professional soldiers to fight for him.

FOOD

 nights were fighting men, so they had to be fit and strong. Like all nobles, they ate lots of meat and fish, but very few vegetables. Wild boar, peacock, and even whale might be served at a feast!

THE LORD'S TABLE

Cows, sheep, pigs, chickens, pheasants, and partridges were kept on the manor to provide meat for the household. The ducks, geese, swans, and other waterfowl that lived on rivers and ponds within the estate would also end up on the lord's table. On holy days, when eating meat was forbidden by the Church, all kinds of fish were eaten.

THE HALL

The whole household ate together in the hall. Instead of plates, everyone except the nobles was given a thick slab of coarse bread, called a trencher, to place their meat on. When the bread had become soggy with gravy, it was thrown to the dogs, or given to the poor.

The lord and his family ate from silver platters, and sat at a raised table at one end of the hall. The less important you were, the farther away you would sit from the lord and the salt

cellar that marked the division between the nobles and the common people. As a knight, you would sit "above the salt."

PASS THE SALT

In medieval times, the best way to stop meat from rotting was to preserve it in salt. To make the meat taste better, cooks added garlic, onions, mustard, and garden herbs to their dishes. In the lord's household, the cook would also have exotic spices like black pepper, cloves, ginger, and nutmeg that came from distant lands and were very expensive.

With their meat, nobles had fine white bread made from wheat flour. Peasants had to make do with coarse, dark bread, and vegetables, which, apart from cabbages and onions, were thought unfit to be served at a knight's table. As a treat, peasants might have an egg or a little bacon.

Cooks prepare a sumptuous feast at a noble household

TABLE MANNERS

In the middle ages, it was important to have good table manners! Follow these rules, and you'll always be welcome at the lord's table:

• Do not put your fingers in your ears
• Do not scratch your head, or any other part of your body
• Do not dip your fingers into the dish at the same time as your neighbor
• Do not poke around in the dish looking for the best bits
• Do not put meat or fish bones back in the dish—drop them on the floor
• Do not eat with dirty hands
• Do not belch in your neighbor's ear

DINNER AT THE CASTLE

FIRST COURSE

Broiled venison,
heron, pheasant, fried pig's head,
and quinces

SECOND COURSE

Partridges, grape-stuffed boiled chicken,
Spit-roasted rabbits with sauce and crushed pine nuts,
Spit-roasted songbirds with lemon sauce,
blanc-mange, pears in wine syrup

HONEY TOASTS WITH PINE NUTS

In the Middle Ages, people kept bees for honey. Here's a medieval recipe using honey, exotic spices, and nuts.

WHAT YOU WILL NEED:

• 8 oz (225 g) honey
• a pinch of ground ginger
• a pinch of cinnamon
• a pinch of ground black pepper
• 4 large square slices of thick white bread, crusts removed
• ½ oz (15 g) pine nuts

1. Place the honey, spices and pepper in a small saucepan over a very low heat. Melt the honey and simmer gently for 2 minutes. Remove from the heat and let cool.
2. Toast the bread lightly on both sides. Cut each slice into small squares.
3. Place on warmed plates, and pour the honey over them. Stick pine nuts upright in each piece. Serve while still warm and eat with a spoon, the way knights used to.

KNIGHTLY PASTIMES

hen knights were not fighting, training, or competing in a tournament, they liked to hunt, dance, and play games. Hunting could be as energetic and dangerous as going into battle.

HUNTING AND HAWKING

obles enjoyed hunting all kinds of animals, because the chase was exciting and good practice for war. Kings and wealthy lords laid aside vast areas of forest, woodland and scrub for hunting deer and wild boar. Knights on horseback would gallop after the deer, shooting arrows at them. Sometimes huntsmen with dogs drove the animal toward the waiting knights. One of the fiercest animals to hunt was the wild boar, and it took a brave knight to face it with only a spear.

Often the lord's household—including the ladies—would accompany the hunters, and there would be feasting and dancing at the end of the day.

Villagers were forbidden to hunt the lord's animals, and if a poacher was caught with even a rabbit

he would be severely punished.

Falconry and hawking were also popular. The hawks were trained to catch wildfowl that could be served at dinner. Good birds were valuable, and it was a serious crime to steal them or their eggs.

This entertainer has dressed as a bishop!

ACROBATS AND MINSTRELS

At dinner, the lord and his household would be entertained by acrobats, jugglers, fire-eaters, and comedians. Minstrels told funny stories, recited poetry, and sang songs accompanied by fiddles, harps, bagpipes, hurdy-gurdies, and other instruments. Minstrels traveled from court to court, so they would often bring exciting news and gossip from other parts of the country.

Hunting was a chance for knights to practice using a longbow

Sometimes, as a surprise, the lord entered the hall in disguise, performed a mime and disappeared again.

DANCING AND GAMES

Musicians playing a hurdy-gurdy and bagpipes

Dancing was a good opportunity for knights to court the ladies! In the ring dance, everyone held hands and danced in a large circle. In another dance, couples danced together then changed partners.

There were also games to play, like "hoodman blind," in which a blindfolded person had to catch and identify the others. Knights enjoyed games of strategy like checkers (draughts), backgammon, and chess. Chess was introduced to Europe from the Middle East, probably by knights returning from the crusades. Noble ladies liked to play board games, too.

MAKING A BOARD GAME
Make your own checkerboard and pieces

WHAT YOU WILL NEED:

- Thick cardboard, 41 x 41 cm (16 x 16 in)
- Pencil
- Ruler
- Marker pen
- Thin cardboard
- Coin
- Scissors
- Paints or crayons

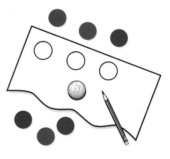

1. Using your ruler, make pencil marks along the edges of the board, one inch apart. Join up the lines along and across the board, to form a checker pattern. With a marker pen, color in alternate squares.

2. Choose a coin small enough to fit inside the squares. On the second piece of cardboard, trace around the coin 24 times. Cut out the circles you have drawn. Paint 12 one color and the rest a second color. Draw animals, mythical beasts or soldiers on the reverse of each of the pieces.

TOURNAMENTS

ournaments began in the eleventh century as training for war. Early contests were extremely violent, but gradually they turned into elaborate spectacles, filled with pageantry and color.

THE TOURNEY

ournaments often lasted several days and included various contests that reflected the way war was fought. The "tourney" was a mock battle between two teams of mounted knights that originally took place in an open field. The knights charged with their lances, then struck out with their swords. The weapons were sharp, just like in war. Foot soldiers were sometimes there to help protect knights who fell and were set upon by opponents. A knight who was captured had to hand over

Two teams use blunt swords and clubs in this tourney

THE DIARY OF ROBERT FITZWILLIAM, SQUIRE, AGED 18 YEARS

MONDAY

My master, Sir Richard of Newbury, is going to a tournament and his armor must be clean and bright. I cleaned his coat of mail in the usual way by kicking it around in a barrel of sand. That was fun, but polishing his armor is hard work and makes my arms ache.

TUESDAY

Today we rode to the tournament. I had packed all the armor in leather bags, along with spare horseshoes and nails. Nigel the page rode the great war-horse and nearly lost control of him, which isn't surprising since his feet barely reach the stirrups. That stallion cost a fortune and Nigel will be flogged if it comes to any harm. Arrived! There are colorful tents everywhere.

WEDNESDAY

Sir Richard answered five challenges to joust and broke four lances. His helm nearly came off during one pass, and his opponent's horse ran wide at another. We did not win anything, though Sir Richard flirted with one of the ladies in the balcony who had given him her sleeve to wear in the contests.

THURSDAY

We took part in the tourney. It was just like a battle, except that the weapons weren't sharp. At one point three knights attacked my master and he would have been unhorsed if I hadn't galloped up and hauled him upright again. I was injured when a sword skidded off my helmet and cut my cheek. Sir Richard stitched up the wound. It's still painful and it looks awful. I hope it doesn't fester.

FRIDAY

Home again, and I have to get on with my practicing. I spent hours hacking at a wooden post with a sword to improve my muscles and my aim. Some of the younger squires are having a tough time since that bullying thug Sir Henry Wakefield arrived. Walter, squire to Edward FitzPayne, fell and badly broke his leg. He is crippled, and might even die. What bad luck. I've seen boys who could not make the grade and were kicked out, but Walter was doing so well.

SATURDAY

Lord Robert, who holds the castle, will knight several of us tomorrow. We all ate in style. Dinner was splendid. It began at 11 o'clock as usual, but lasted into the afternoon because there were three courses instead of two. I was able to show off by carving the roast beef for my master in front of the others. One of the serving men tripped over a dog and sent the whole lot flying, for which he was soundly cuffed, but the diners thought it was funny. My lord brought his minstrels with him, and they sang romance songs about King Arthur.

SUNDAY

What a day! Despite spending all night in the chapel keeping vigil with my sword at the altar, I was too excited to be tired. I was bathed this morning and dressed in special clothes. Gold knightly spurs were fitted to my heels, then Lord Robert buckled on my sword and gave me the accolade on the shoulder, instructing me to uphold the knightly virtues. I will do my best.

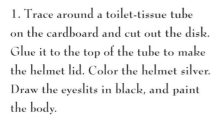

A JOUSTING KNIGHT

Make two jousting knights, and have a tournament!

WHAT YOU WILL NEED: Scissors •Ruler •Glue
•Tape •Poster paints •Metallic markers

THE KNIGHT:

- Toilet-tissue roll tube
- Black marker
- Plastic straw
- Fabric
- Cardboard

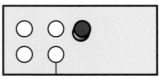

1. Trace around a toilet-tissue tube on the cardboard and cut out the disk. Glue it to the top of the tube to make the helmet lid. Color the helmet silver. Draw the eyeslits in black, and paint the body.

2. Paint the straw. Make two holes in the knight's right side and thread the straw through. Fasten a piece of fabric around the body, making a small cut for the lance to pass through.

3. Make a shield from cardboard and decorate it in heraldic colors. Glue it to the knight's left side. Tape the knight to the saddle, and he's ready to joust!

THE HORSE:

- Thin cardboard
- Toilet-tissue tube
- 4 soda bottle tops
- 2 plastic straws
- Paper

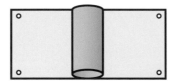

1. Cut a strip of cardboard as wide as the toilet-tissue tube and 20 cm (8 in) long. This will be the horse's "trapper." Decorate it in heraldic colors. Make a big hole at each corner. Glue the tube in the center of the cardboard strip.

3. Thread two straws through the holes in the trapper. Push the ends through the cardboard disks. Cut slits in the ends of each straw, open them out and tape down. Push the disks into the bottle tops.

2. On cardboard, draw around the bottle tops and cut out four disks. Make a hole in the middle of the disks and trim them to fit inside the bottle tops.

4. On cardboard, draw and color a horse's head and neck and cut it out. Tape it inside the tube. Make a tail from snipped paper. Paint a saddle for the knight to sit on.

his horse and armor to the victor. Fortunes could be made and lost by knights who were prepared to risk their honor and their lives.

THE JOUST

By the thirteenth century, knights were beginning to take part in a one-to-one contest called a "joust." In a joust, one knight charged at another with a lance and tried to knock him from his horse. The joust was held in a large arena called the "lists" surrounded by spectators and watched by judges who awarded points. It was much easier to see the action at a joust than at a tourney, where it was often hard to tell what was going on. Knights could now display their skill with the lance with less risk of being fatally injured. Blunt weapons were often used, but injuries still happened, and in the fifteenth century a barrier called the "tilt" was introduced to separate the competing horsemen. Foot combats were sometimes included.

Two knights display their skill at foot combat

CHANGING TIMES

The Church disapproved of knights fighting each other for fun, and by the fifteenth century tournaments had become less warlike and more lavish and entertaining. Brightly dressed heralds delivered challenges, and rules of combat were agreed by both sides. Competing knights in shining armor paraded with colorful crests attached to their helmets, and ladies gave scarves to their favorites.

CHIVALRY

C hivalry is the name for the code of honor that all knights were expected to follow. This code grew out of friendships between knights, and respect for the Church. Chivalry influenced literature and life at court.

A troubadour

BAD MANNERS

A knight pledges his love to a lady

K nights were members of the nobility—which included kings, dukes and barons—but they were also rough fighting men who could be greedy and cruel. Invading knights sometimes killed peasants, robbed houses and slaughtered people when they conquered a town. Churchmen were worried about knights' bad behavior, and in the eleventh century they tried to stop knights from fighting on certain days of the week! However, knights who had trained together as boys, and fought side by side, developed a bond of friendship and loyalty that the Church decided to encourage.

COURTLY LOVE

In the twelfth century, worship of the Virgin Mary became common, and courteous behavior was now expected by a knight toward his lady. Poems about this courteous behavior, or "courtly love," became fashionable, and spread from the south of France to the rest of Europe. Minstrels called "troubadours" traveled from court to court singing sad love poems, in which the gallant lover hardly ever won the hand of his beautiful lady. In reality, knights still married rich women they didn't love just to get hold of their land.

King Arthur slays a giant with his sword, Excalibur

EPICS AND ROMANCES

Early knights had enjoyed epic poems about fierce battles, but these were overtaken by "romances" that had everything: fighting, love, magic, and adventure. A popular subject for romances was the story of King Arthur and the knights of the Round Table.

KING ARTHUR

King Arthur lived in a great palace with his loyal band of knights. Troubadours told how Arthur and knights like Sir Gawain and Sir Lancelot left the court at Camelot to search for the Holy Grail—a cup used by Jesus at the Last Supper—fighting monsters and giants on the way.

ARE YOU A CHIVALROUS KNIGHT?

Lots of stories are told about St. George fighting dragons and rescuing ladies. Do you have what it takes to be a knight in shining armor?

1. You come across a maiden about to be eaten by a dragon.
DO YOU:
A Take the dragon home and feed it?
B Go for help?
C Slay the dragon with your sword?

2. A giant challenges you to a duel.
DO YOU:
A Sing him a calming lullaby?
B Run up a tree and hide?
C Fetch your longest sword or lance?

ANSWERS:
Both As: You are too kind-hearted to make it as a knight. Consider a career as a troubadour.
Both Bs: You are very sensible, and would do a good job of managing the lord's estate.
Both Cs: Well done! You are brave and fearless, and should be knighted right away.

A KNIGHTLY CODE OF HONOR

Here's a code of chivalry for all good knights to try and follow.

Rule One
Believe in the Church and obey her teachings

Rule Two
Always obey your feudal overlord, so long as those duties do not conflict with the duties of God

Rule Three
Respect and pity the weak, and be steadfast in defending them

Rule Four
Love your country

Rule Five
Refuse to retreat before the enemy

Rule Six
Be courteous toward women

Rule Seven
Be loyal to truth and to the pledged word

Rule Eight
Be generous in giving

Rule Nine
Champion the right and the good, in every place and at all times, against the forces of evil

THE CRUSADES

he most famous crusades were wars waged by Christians to recapture Jerusalem from the Muslims. Knights joined the thousands of ordinary men and women who went to the Holy Land to fight.

THE PILGRIMS

In the Middle Ages, most of the people in western Europe belonged to the Catholic Church, whose leader was the pope. For many years, popes had encouraged their followers to go on journeys, called "pilgrimages," to holy places. The longest and most difficult pilgrimage was to Jerusalem, the place where Jesus was killed.

In the eleventh century, Pope Urban II became worried when Turkish Muslims began attacking pilgrims to Jerusalem. The pope called upon Christians to capture the city and make it safe again.

The Muslims, on the left, don't wear any armor, and fight with long curved swords

THE FIRST CRUSADE

In 1096, thousands of ordinary people obeyed the pope's call, leaving their homes and families to journey to the Holy Land. They traveled across Europe on foot, and many of them died of starvation and disease along the way.

The crosses on this knight's surcoat show that he is a crusader

THE CRUSADER KNIGHT

Knights from all over Europe also became crusaders. A knight who had taken a vow to fight for the Church had a cross sewn onto his surcoat, but still dressed in mail and carried a sword. When traveling, his armor would be carefully wrapped and carried on the back of a pack horse or in a cart.

BUILDING A SIEGE CATAPULT

Crusading knights used catapults to hurl huge stones at the walls of enemy castles. Use this model catapult to fire balls of scrunched-up paper at a target—never at another person.

WHAT YOU WILL NEED:

- Plastic spoon
- Shoe box
- Pencil
- Ruler
- Scissors
- Paint
- Thick rubber band
- Two kitchen matches with the ends cut off. Ask an adult for help with this.

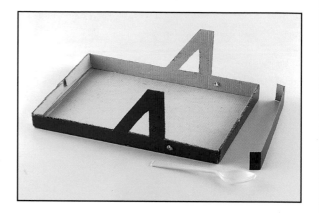

1. Hold the spoon handle against the shoe box and make a pencil mark about 2.5 cm (1 in) from the end of the spoon. Make a hole, then do the same on the other side.

Cut away the sides leaving the triangular shape shown in the picture. Make the base 2.5 cm (1 in) all around. Cut a strip from the box lid. Glue this to the two side pieces.

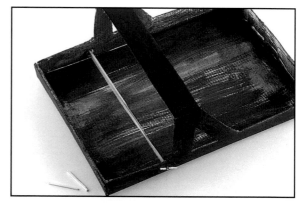

2. Paint the frame brown to look like wood. Thread the ends of the rubber band through the holes and keep them in place with the matches.

3. Push the spoon handle through the rubber band. Twist the matches forward, forcing the spoon up against the crossbar.

To fire the catapult, pull back the spoon, load it, and let go.

JERUSALEM

After a long siege, Jerusalem was captured by the Christians in 1099. The crusaders had been successful because the Muslims were busy fighting each other. However, in the twelfth century, a new leader, whose name was Saladin, united all the Muslims and retook Jerusalem.

On this map, the city of Jerusalem is placed at the center of the world

RICHARD THE LIONHEART

A new crusade was proclaimed, and one of its leaders was King Richard I of England. He joined the French king, and besieged a city called Acre. Richard promised Saladin that everyone in Acre would be freed if the city was handed over to the Christians. But when Saladin surrendered, Richard behaved very badly and ordered hundreds of Muslim captives to be slaughtered.

Richard then marched his troops toward Jerusalem, but knowing that he wouldn't be able to hold the city even if he managed to capture it, he decided to turn back. He sailed for England, but was shipwrecked on the way and captured by Germans. Richard spent nearly two years in prison before a ransom was paid and he was allowed to return home.

WARRIOR MONKS

Pilgrims continued to visit the Holy Land, so a band of fighting monks was formed to protect them. They were called the Knights Templar, and they were based in Jerusalem. Another band of monks, called the Hospitallers, ran hospitals and cared for sick pilgrims. These monks were also fighting men, and they built great castles as well as hospitals.

The last leaders of the Knights Templar were burned at the stake by their Christian enemies